JOURNEY TO STONEHENGE

BY FRED GRAVER

ILLUSTRATED BY LESLIE MORRILL

An R.A. Montgomery Book

BANTAM BOOKS

TORONTO · NEW YORK · LONDON · SYDNEY · AUCKLAND

RL 5, IL age 10 and up

JOURNEY TO STONEHENGE
A Bantam Book / August 1984

CHOOSE YOUR OWN ADVENTURE® is a registered trademark of
Bantam Books, Inc. Registered in U.S. Patent and Trademark
Office and elsewhere.
Original conception of Edward Packard.
Front cover art by Ralph Reese.

ISBN 0-553-24484-1

Published simultaneously in the United States and Canada

Bantam Books are published by Bantam Books, Inc. Its trademark, consisting of the words "Bantam Books" and the por-
trayal of a rooster, is Registered in U.S. Patent and Trademark
Office and in other countries. Marca Registrada. Bantam
Books, Inc., 666 Fifth Avenue, New York, New York 10103.

PRINTED IN THE UNITED STATES OF AMERICA

O   0 9 8 7 6 5 4 3 2 1

JOURNEY TO
STONEHENGE

WARNING!!!

Do not read this book straight through from beginning to end! These pages contain many different adventures you can have as you journey through time at Stonehenge. As you read along you will be asked to make decisions and choices. The adventures you have will be the result of the decisions you make. *You* are responsible because *you* choose! After you make a choice, follow the instructions to see what happens to you next.

Think carefully before you make a move. If you're lucky, you could unravel the secrets of Stonehenge. Or you could become lost in its mystery.

SPECIAL WARNING!!!

You will be traveling to Stonehenge as a reporter. Before you go, you may want to read the briefing that your newspaper has prepared. This information about the building of Stonehenge could provide the background you need to help you in your travels. The briefing, if you choose to read it, begins on the next page.

BRIEFING ON STONEHENGE

Stonehenge is a great monument constructed of earth and stone by primitive civilizations in Britain. No one knows exactly why Stonehenge was built, who built it, or what purpose it served once it was completed.

Many believe that Stonehenge was used to observe the cycles of the sun and moon, and to aid ancient people in planting and harvesting. Others feel that it provided a central meeting place for tribes—a place for worship, for making laws, and for marketing crops and goods.

Perhaps the greatest puzzle of all is *how* Stonehenge was built. How were these huge stones transported to this site? How were they carved, fitted to each other, and raised in the enormous arches we now call trilithons?

We will never know the answers to these questions. The culture that built Stonehenge is gone forever, leaving no trace of itself other than this monument, only part of which is standing today.

Scientists *do* know approximately when Stonehenge was built: between the years 2800 and 1400 B.C., in three separate stages. The first stage saw the completion of the circular hill, which we know as the outermost circle of Stonehenge, and the three circles of holes, fifty-six in all, that ring the monument. The four "station stones," which were supposedly used to indicate the positions of the moon at various times of the year, also were constructed during this first stage.

The second stage, which began in 2100 B.C., saw the construction of the double circle of standing stones at the center of the monument, as well as the broad avenue that leads to Stonehenge from the outer edge of the grassy plains surrounding it.

In the third, final, stage, the double circle of stones was actually taken apart and rebuilt, and many of the trilithons were erected.

It's a good thing to remember, as you ponder the mysteries of Stonehenge, that fourteen hundred years is a long time—seven times as long, for example, as the history of the United States. In that time, different tribes and chiefdoms contributed to the construction of Stonehenge. Each may have had very different reasons for building the monument. Perhaps one day we will know what these reasons were. Perhaps, in *your* journey to Stonehenge, you will discover some of them.

You are in the office of *Tightwire,* a newspaper written by, for, and about kids all over the world. The editor in chief, your friend Mark, hands you a cablegram.

TEEN-AGE ARCHEOLOGISTS ARE WORKING AT STONEHENGE UNDER MY LEADERSHIP. NEW DISCOVERIES, PHENOMENA WILL STARTLE THE WORLD. SEND REPORTER WITHIN FIVE DAYS.

—*P. J. Engleton*

Turn to page 2.

"Sounds like a crackpot to me," you say to Mark.

"I checked him out," Mark replies. "He's the real thing. Fifteen years old, but a brilliant student of history and archeology. He and a group of other British kids convinced their government to let them dig around Stonehenge this summer— the first group in ten years to get permission. Even if his discoveries don't startle the world, there's a story in Stonehenge and his group. Want to go?"

"Why not?" you answer. "I've never been to England. It should be fun."

That night, you're on a jet to London. Mark has cabled P. J. Engleton to expect you, and when you arrive, you're greeted by a young woman.

"I'm Joanne, and I'm working with P.J.," she tells you. "My car is outside."

Go on to the next page.

On the long drive through the English countryside, Joanne fills you in on P.J. and his expedition. "P.J. is a child prodigy and a genius, although I'd say he's a self-proclaimed one. Very simply, he's a publicity hound."

"Do you think he exaggerated to get me here?" you ask.

"Well, yes and no," Joanne answers. "P.J.'s made some wild claims. He says he's witnessing some very strange things around Stonehenge . . . things that have to do with, as he puts it, 'a breakdown in the walls of space and time.'" Taking her eyes from the road, Joanne turns to get your reaction before continuing, "The problem is, no one else seems to know exactly what he's talking about. He's alone most of the time. You'll see what I mean."

Turn to page 6.

Not daring to leave P.J. alone, you follow him into the circle. As you near the center of Stonehenge, you feel yourself being pulled by a force beyond your power.

Inside the inner ring, the massive stones seem to hover over the ground. The singing is louder now. Hundreds of voices chant in a language you've never heard. Somehow, though, you feel that you can understand it.

In front of the altar stone, you see three rocks, each about the size of a golf ball, glowing with a rainbowlike light. As you follow P.J. toward them, you sense that the voices are trapped within these rocks. P.J. edges closer. Slowly the stones lift from the ground, and the two end stones begin to revolve around the middle one.

There's a story here—if you live to tell it! Even so, it might be smart to forget the story and run in the other direction. Just as you think this, P.J. reaches for the middle stone. For a moment he stands motionless. Then he holds his hand out to you.

If you grab P.J.'s hand and try to pull him out, turn to page 51.

If you grab one of the stones yourself, turn to page 7.

You're not going after P.J. unprepared. Carefully, making sure that no one sees you, you sneak into the equipment tent and pack a small knapsack with food, cooking utensils, and a water pouch. Then you head for Stonehenge.

As you enter the inner circle you hear the singing and chanting again, although there's no sign of P.J. All around you, the stones and rocks are bathed with rainbow-colored light, as if the moonlight had been passed through a prism. As you walk toward the altar stone, the singing becomes louder.

Turn to page 10.

At last you and Joanne reach Stonehenge. Dark clouds fly low in the sky and a cool breeze sweeps the plain as you walk up the broad avenue leading to the monument. The first thing you notice are several groups of students, all working intently, around the monument. Then you look up at the monoliths of Stonehenge. Immediately you are struck by the grace and simplicity of these enormous stones.

You enter Stonehenge through a break in the earthwork—a mound of earth which circles the rings of stones. Just inside the mound are three rings of holes, most of which have been covered with slabs of white slate. Beyond those three circles stand the massive, towering stones which are the megalith Stonehenge. In the center of it all, standing in solitude and power, is the altar stone.

Turn to page 8.

You reach for one of the end stones. It is cool in your hand, and when you touch it your skin takes on its rainbow tint. All around you everything seems to be lifting, shaking, rising from the ground. Suddenly, you are hurled into the air, whirling around the stones as if on a prehistoric merry-go-round.

The voices continue to chant and sing, and the light becomes brighter and brighter. A thousand different colors explode in your mind. You become dizzy. Then you lose consciousness.

Turn to page 12.

"Hello, Yank," a boisterous voice calls from behind you. "My name is P. J. Engleton." P.J., a chubby English youth, takes you aside, leaving Joanne behind. "Nice of you to come. I was thinking—if you want the real story about Stonehenge, you'd best stay in my tent with me. Now think it over, there's no rush. But you wouldn't regret it." As quickly as the conversation began, it ends, as P.J. walks away from you.

"That means he's finished talking," Joanne says, coming up beside you. "Why don't I show you to the guest tent?"

"Well, P.J. mentioned something about staying with him," you say.

"Hey, what kind of reporter *are* you?" Joanne exclaims. "How do you expect to get an objective picture of this expedition, staying with one of its members? It's up to you, of course, but I'd stay on my own if I were you. At least until you get a better idea of what we're all about."

If you decide to stay in the guest tent,
turn to page 56.

If you decide to stay with P.J.,
turn to page 16.

Before you, three small stones glowing with multicolored light are lying on the ground. You don't quite believe it, but the voices seem to be trapped inside the stones. Slowly, the three small stones lift from the ground and begin to revolve around each other. You grab for one of them.

As you hold the stone in your hand, your skin becomes tinted with the same rainbow color that surrounds you. Your body rises from the ground and, suddenly, you are hurled around Stonehenge. The singing grows louder and louder, and the lights and voices seem to fill your head. Faster

and faster you spin, until you become so dizzy you lose consciousness.

When you wake up, you are seated on a small mound of dirt, overlooking a long racing track. Immediately you recognize it as the cursus that extends over the hills and valleys near Stonehenge.

Turn to page 42.

When you wake up, you feel cold and wet all over. Your face and hands are covered with mud. And your clothes have changed completely! Now you're wearing a large, bulky cloth tunic, woven from a very coarse material that feels like burlap. Your bare feet are clad in leather sandals. At your side, hanging from a leather thong, is a small pouch. You reach inside and feel the three stones.

You scramble to your feet. You are standing on a muddy riverbank. Farther up the river you see a group of men working. Some are pulling wooden pontoons loaded with enormous stones up onto the river bank. Others are transferring the stones from the pontoons onto log carriers. Long, braided leather straps are used in place of rope. The work appears clumsy, difficult, and grueling.

Two of the men break off from the work group and begin walking toward you. As they get closer you can hear them talking. Although they are speaking in a strange language, you understand everything they say!

If you decide to ask the men for help,
turn to page 21.

If you decide to hide and try to overhear them,
turn to page 104.

"See you tomorrow," you call to the boy, and begin walking along a dirt path that leads uphill through a forest. For some time, you follow the path. Evening falls, and it becomes quite dark. You turn around, but in the darkness you lose your way. You're no longer on the path leading back to Stonehenge.

Finally, you find your way out of the forest and back to Stonehenge. Light is just breaking over the horizon. You have walked all night. As you enter the monument area you hear voices. Two men stand talking. One is very tall, with a thick red beard. The other man is short and wiry, wearing a heavy pouch at his side.

"They will attack tonight, Osin," the tall man says, "unless you can find some other way."

"An attack would be disastrous, Beltan. The Huntsmen would lose many lives. I am sure that if I were given more time I could come up with a better way to defeat the Priestess."

"Time is of the essence," proclaims Beltan. "Once the Priestess begins to hold her rituals here, the people will gather under her. Do not forget—we have been promised great wealth from the Warlord of the Huntsmen if we can stop that from happening."

Turn to page 76.

"P.J.?" you whisper.

"I can't believe it!" P.J. answers. "We've been sent back in time through those stones. We're occupying the bodies of two people from this time! Do you have the stones?"

"The healers took them from me. We've got to get them back somehow."

Just then, a stunningly beautiful woman enters the room. "You will get your stones back," she says. "As soon as my astronomers finish studying them." She holds her hands out to you. "Welcome to the Ring of the Moon. I am the Priestess of the Moon Tribe. You realize, of course, that you are not the first people to journey through time through the power of the moon. Unfortunately, you've chosen a very bad time to do so. We are involved in a war with the Huntsmen, a tribe trying to destroy us *and* our ring. I would hope that you can be saved from the fighting, but I am afraid I cannot ensure your safety."

Turn to page 20.

"I'll take my chances with P.J.," you tell
Joanne.

"Suit yourself," she says. "I think you're making a big mistake."

That night, after everyone has gone to sleep,
P.J. is still awake. "There's something at the
monument I want you to see," he whispers. "Follow me."

You rush out after him. "I've been witnessing
paranormal disturbances over the last few
nights," P.J. tells you as you walk toward the
monument. "I'd like you to observe them with
me."

He leads you to a place just outside the earthen
ring surrounding Stonehenge. "Watch the monument," he says, laying a sleeping bag on the
ground. "If anything happens, wake me."

In no time at all, P.J. is asleep. Hours pass. You
watch as the moon weaves a path through the
stones and arches of Stonehenge. Suddenly you
hear noises coming from the inner rings of the
monument! It sounds as if a group of people are
inside, chanting a strange language. You turn to
wake P.J., but he is already sitting bolt upright, his
eyes wide open as if in a daze.

Go on to the next page.

"P.J., what's going on here?" you ask. He doesn't answer. Instead he gets up and walks toward the monument. You turn to watch him and see a colored light glowing within Stonehenge. It's as if the moon had been cast through a prism, bathing the stones in a spectrum of light. P.J. is moving as though he were hypnotized. He walks into the circle of light. Goose bumps prickle your flesh, and a chill goes down your spine. You don't know what to do. All you know is that you've never been this afraid before.

If you follow P.J. into the circle, turn to page 4.

If you run back to the camp to get help, turn to page 80.

The battle over Stonehenge is quick but bloody. With their solid formation and crowded charge, the Beakers are an easy target for the defending Huntsmen. Many Beakers die, and the survivors soon call retreat. In the afternoon sun an uneasy quiet settles over the area.

Then, as the sun dips into the horizon, the Beakers are back! With incredible fierceness they storm Stonehenge from every side. This time they catch the Huntsmen by surprise and drive them from the monument.

As night falls you remain on the hill overlooking Stonehenge and watch the Beakers prepare the funeral ritual for their dead. They build an enormous fire and cremate the bodies of the fallen soldiers. When the fire has consumed the bodies, the Beakers take the bones of the dead and bury them in holes surrounding Stonehenge. Finally, into each hole, they place the pieces of the dead person's broken beaker, as if the vessel had somehow held the person's soul.

Watching this ritual, you begin to sense the power that Stonehenge has for these people. Here is where they have placed their hearts and souls. Here is where their dead come to rest, and where the living come to sense the harmony of all life.

Turn to page 22.

Suddenly you hear screaming and shouting outside. A guard rushes in and yells, "The Huntsmen are attacking! Take your positions!" He rushes from the room as quickly as he entered, with the Priestess following him.

"What positions?" asks P.J.

"Beats me," you answer. "But if we go out there, we'll get killed for sure. Let's hide."

You and P.J. take cover behind a large altar. The battle outside rages on for several hours. Finally the noise of fighting dies down. You and P.J. come out of hiding and are met by an angry Starn.

"What cowards," he sneers. "Do not think I failed to notice that you never entered the battle. I should turn you in to the guard now, but I will give you one more chance. The Huntsmen have captured the Priestess, and a raiding party is being formed to rescue her. You can either join it, or stay here and defend the fortress."

P.J. leans over and whispers in your ear. "He thinks we're from this time. We'd better go along with him for now. You decide what we should do, but let's do *something* before he has our heads taken off!"

If you join the raiding party, turn to page 63.

If you choose to stay and defend the fortress, turn to page 87.

You walk toward the two men. "Please, I am far from my home, and lost. Can you help me?" you call out.

One of the men looks at you with amazement; then his surprise turns to sharp anger. He yanks a dagger from his belt. "Beaker!" he yells. You don't know what "beaker" means, but you know enough to turn and run. "We have found a Beaker!" he yells.

You race away, leaving the men far behind. Breathless, you cut inland to the nearby forest, where you follow a rutted path. The path leads to a clearing dotted with small fires.

Night is falling, so you stop by the clearing, watching the people camped within. There seems to be one family to each fire. Each group has its own meal, and each person has his own thick stone mug.

Suddenly you begin to laugh. Of course! These people are drinking from *beakers*, the word you use for containers in a chemistry lab. Perhaps they will be more help than the others, who chased you.

You enter the Beaker camp, this time using a different strategy than you did with the two men on the river bank. Rushing into the camp, you yell, "Help! The people near the stone ring are after me! Help me!"

Turn to page 99.

When the ceremony has ended, you emerge from your hiding place and walk to Stonehenge's inner ring. You remove the three stones from your pouch and prepare to travel again in time. Holding the stones in your hand, you take one more look around, trying to remember all that you see. There is more than a simple news story here—you could devote your life to telling the story of the world you've seen.

The End

Very quietly, you leave the camp and walk toward Stonehenge. The night is still, and the moon hangs brightly in the sky.

From the earthen ring, you watch in amazement as Joanne enters Stonehenge. She walks as if in a daze. As you follow her into the ring of stones, you see someone approaching her—the young man in your dream? Joanne reaches for him, but he moves away from her and begins to run. She chases after him. Suddenly he stops and whirls around. With a wave of his arm, both he and Joanne disappear!

The next day, Joanne is nowhere to be found. You try to explain to everyone what occurred the night before, but no one believes you.

After news of Joanne's disappearance reaches London, the student group is forced to leave Stonehenge. When you return to the United States, you file your story with *Tightwire*. Mark reads it carefully, then says, "Well, I'll run everything but that silly part about your dream and that girl vanishing before your eyes. You can't expect anyone to believe *that*, can you?"

The End

A Beaker girl picks you up and takes you to a nearby hillside. There, she binds your wounds, gives you something to drink that eases your pain, and returns to the fighting. You watch the

battle raging, content at seeing many of your strategies working. You feel very close to these people at this moment, and wish earnestly for their victory.

Turn to page 28.

Hoping no one notices, you edge away from the track. An older woman grabs your arm. "What are you doing, Kelb?" she asks angrily. "You will disgrace our tribe. Get back there."

"I can't run," you say. "You must send in another. I feel weak, and cannot run with honor."

The woman glares at you. "Then go find your cousin Aus. He will give you something to do."

You don't know where to find Aus, so you go back to the place where you had been sitting. Picking up your pack, you look up to see another athlete taking your place in the race. Suddenly, you hear a voice behind you.

"Where have you been?" a young man asks. "I thought you were supposed to see me after you dropped out of the race."

You realize that this must be Aus, your cousin. "I was just coming over there," you say.

"Well, there is no need to. I have brought you your mask and shield." He hands you a mask of a bearded man, and a tunic with a shield embroidered on it. "Watch the races on the cursus, and then meet us at sunset for the ceremony."

Turn to page 108.

You tell yourself that if P.J. needs you, he has the power to get you. Sure enough, late that night a guard pounds on Mera's door. "The chief wants the young friend staying with you," he barks.

The guard leads you to the inner ring of Stonehenge, where P.J. stands in front of a large tripod, on which are mounted a variety of stones, jewels, and bronze pieces.

"I will show you how we punish traitors," P.J. tells the guard. He winks at you, and you realize this is a necessary deception. P.J. approaches you. "I'm not going back," he whispers.

"What do you mean?" you ask, startled.

"I think I'm going to be very happy here. These people have become like family to me. This is good work, building Stonehenge. I want to stay. Take these back."

With that, P.J. hands you some daggers, cups, and medallions. Then he leads you to the middle of the tripod. You step inside, and a thunderclap sends you reeling through time.

Turn to page 30.

The battle rages on in the dwindling moments of the day. You have told the Beakers to wait until the sunlight is just fading to make their last, most powerful, attack on the Huntsmen. And this is what they do. The Beakers fight valiantly, using their spears, bows and arrows, and slingshots. Eventually, the Beakers invade Stonehenge, running the Huntsmen out.

Over the next few days, your leg heals under the careful eyes of the Beakers. You get to know Lura, the girl who first looked after you, a little better. "I have no home of my own," she says quietly. "My family died many months ago in another battle with the Huntsmen."

"My family and home are far, far away," you say, and then tell Lura the story of your trip through time. As you explain, Lura's eyes become wide with excitement.

Turn to page 34.

The girl's blade presses against your throat. "I don't know who the Beakers are," you say, "but if you take that thing away, I'll tell you a secret. Just back away a few steps."

The girl eyes you suspiciously but does as you ask, still holding the spear toward you. You pull the stones from your pouch. "With these stones, I can travel through time. I traveled here by the magic in these stones. All I really want to do is return. Can you help me?"

The girl says nothing but, prodding you with her spear, leads you into the camp. You pass huts, campfires, and small families gathered in the outdoors. Finally, the girl leads you to a hut that seems to be her home. She brings you inside and then goes out to speak with her family.

After a while, a man enters the hut. "I am Caleb, father of Tyn, the girl who brought you here. Tyn told me what you said to her on the river bank. I know nothing about the magic that you speak of, but there are many who would be interested in talking with you."

Caleb invites you to stay with his family. You like them and decide to stay for a while.

Turn to page 94.

When you wake up, you are lying in the inner ring of Stonehenge. The items P.J. gave you are gone. You have no idea how long you've been away, but when you walk into camp you find nothing changed. You enter your tent. P.J. is asleep on his cot!

"P.J.," you say, shaking him. "Did you change your mind? How did you get back?"

"Change my mind about what?" P.J. asks sleepily.

You look at each other, confused. P.J. really has no idea of what you're talking about. You keep your silence and wait to see if, maybe, you were only dreaming.

The End

In the village, the Huntsmen are caught in a storm of rocks. Their ranks break in confusion as Starn leads a charge into the fortress. The Huntsmen battle valiantly against the Tribe of the Moon. You fight your way through a band of soldiers until, suddenly, you find yourself face to face with their leader—the vicious Warlord.

With a bloodcurdling scream the Warlord hurls a spiked metal ball at you. Instantly you duck and hurl yourself at his legs, tackling him. The Warlord falls—straight onto Starn's extended spear.

With the death of their Warlord, the injured Huntsmen retreat quickly. When the last of them has fled the village, you, P.J., and Starn turn and head back through the forest to rescue the Priestess.

Turn to page 35.

Joanne and the others seem to take forever to get ready, but finally you all head back to Stonehenge. Passing P.J.'s tent, you see that he's gone.

When you reach the monument, there is nothing to see but the stones in the moonlight. The voices, the colored lights—everything is gone! You return to the camp, mystified.

The next day, you work with a group making preparations for the observation of a lunar eclipse at Stonehenge. Joanne explains the project to you.

"We're monitoring the path of the moon from various angles around Stonehenge," she tells you. "We want to compare our observations, and

see if, in fact, primitive people might have used Stonehenge as an astronomical observatory."

That night, when the eclipse occurs, everything is ready: cameras have been mounted, special light-enclosed recording stations have been built, and each student has a specified area to work in.

Suddenly, P.J. taps your shoulder. "I think there's something you should see," he says.

"Where have you been?" you demand.

"Questions later. Follow me."

Turn to page 68.

"Will you take me back with you?" Lura asks. "I can get you to Stonehenge if you will."

You agree to take Lura into the twentieth century with you, but not before explaining that she will probably have a difficult time living in modern society.

That night, you bring the stones out and wait for them to absorb the power of the moon. Soon the light begins to change, and the singing comes from the stones. Lura grasps your hand, and the two of you wait for the stones to rise and begin spinning. When they do you reach for the middle one, and you and Lura are pulled into the rushing forces of time. As you look down at the Beakers, tears come to your eyes. You will miss these strong, independent people—but you and Lura have a great adventure ahead of you.

The End

The Huntsmen's camp is empty. You begin to rush forward, though Starn tries to hold you back.

As you stoop to enter the tent Starn pointed out earlier, you are hit on the back of the head. With your last ounce of strength, you throw yourself into the tent, where you find the Priestess, bound and gagged.

You struggle to reach the Priestess, but the pain in your head is too great for you to move. Looking into her eyes, you feel as though she is trying to thank you for your brave attempt to save her. Outside, P.J. is yelling for Starn. He screams as the Huntsmen overtake him.

You tried, but it's too late now.

The End

"Let's go back to the fortress," you tell P.J. "There's probably more safety in numbers."

At the forest's edge, overlooking Stonehenge, you join Starn and the rest of the raiders. The Huntsmen within the village are wreaking havoc. Families are being thrown from their homes as each hut is searched for valuables.

Starn signals you to a clump of bushes. When you reach him, he pulls back the branches to reveal a small but powerful catapult. "We hid several of these some time ago," he says. "When I give the signal, our tribesmen will take cover and we will fire the catapults. It will appear that there are many more of us out here than there really are. The Huntsmen will flee if they believe they are outnumbered."

You watch as Starn gives the same instructions to the other raiders. You wait. Then a sharp whistle pierces the air. Starn's signal! You see the tribesmen inside the fortress run for cover. You pull the rope holding the catapult, and watch as your boulder hurtles toward the village.

Turn to page 31.

Time travel! What a story this could make!

You nod to Merlin, and the next thing you know, you're standing in an open field. You recognize it as Stonehenge, but in a very early stage—only the earthen mound and some of the holes have been completed. All around, people are working. Some at the edge of the plain are dragging enormous stones. Closer to the monument, masons are carving the stones. Other workers are struggling to erect the trilithons.

"This is what I want to show you," Merlin begins. "Everything you see here—from the ring of earth to the stones—and even things that you cannot see, such as the earth beneath our feet and what is far below it—contributes to the power of this place. It is a place that can tap the power of the universe as it is stored on this planet. A power that can transcend space and time. But it must not fall into the wrong hands, and that is precisely what I fear is going to happen now." At this, Merlin hangs his head. "Wizards are born with great powers," he tells you, "but they must grow into them. I am still so young. But at least you are here to set the record straight for history."

Go on to the next page.

At that moment, a short man in a cloth tunic approaches Merlin. "Aurelius demands your presence," he barks.

Merlin turns to you, looking worried and flustered. "You must not be seen by Aurelius," he warns. "Wait for me here. I will return shortly."

Merlin walks away, leaving you to watch the hustle and bustle around Stonehenge. Hours pass. Night falls. The workers go home to their small huts in the nearby forest. You are left alone—hungry, thirsty, and a little scared. As the sun sets the air becomes colder. You wonder if Merlin has forgotten you.

If you search for Merlin, turn to page 93.

If you remain where you are, turn to page 48.

You sense that becoming a spy would put you in terrible danger, and it wouldn't help you achieve your ultimate goal—returning to your own time.

"I'm afraid that I'm just not the right person for the job," you tell the men. "You'd be much better off finding someone else."

Beltan peers over at you. "Get out, coward," he says, and pushes you away. Quickly you run from the monument toward the forest. In the cool morning air you wait, shivering, for the workers to begin arriving. A short time later, you hear Osin calling you.

"Auric," he calls. "I know you are in there. Come out—I have something important to tell you."

Slowly you emerge from the forest. As you get closer to Osin he begins to smile. "What I wanted to tell you," he says, "is that you know too much. Goodbye."

At that, he pulls a dagger from his tunic and thrusts it forward. Blackness descends on you as you fall to the ground.

The End

Around you is a crowd of people dressed in brightly colored clothing. Many wear helmets made of animal heads and carry banners atop wooden staffs. This must be some kind of celebration or sporting event. Looking down, you see that you are dressed simply—in a short, loose tunic and leather sandals bound up to your knees. For some reason, though, you're still carrying your pack.

Before you can begin to figure out just how you made this change, a cheer rises from the crowd. In the distance, you see a small group of runners approaching a finish line. They are exhausted, pushing with their last ounce of strength to cross the line. Caught in the excitement, you leap to your feet, and only then, to the south, do you see Stonehenge.

A boy just a little older than you is declared the winner and is surrounded by cheering admirers. But amidst the throng, you notice that the runner who came in last is being dragged away by a pair of guards; his eyes are filled with terror.

Turn to page 46.

"I can't remember where my home is," you say to the boy in his language. "To tell you the truth, I don't even remember my own name."

"Your name is Auric," the boy says. "My name is Starn. We both live in this village and are working on the Ring of the Moon. Perhaps you have been hurt more seriously than we thought. I think we should go see the healers in the Priestess's temple."

Starn leads you back to the ring, to a group of wood-and-mud huts built to the side of Stonehenge. A fortress has been erected around these, and you have to pass through a group of guards on your way to the temple—a large building of stone and colored glass.

Inside the temple, Starn tells a group of women about your fall and loss of memory. They lay you on a slab of rock and take your tool pouch from you. You watch helplessly as they also remove the pouch holding the three stones. The healers begin to tend to your wounds.

"Yours is the second accident today," one of the healers tells you. "Another boy fell and was hurt badly, too. He is in the next room."

In a flash you realize that the other boy could be P.J. You leap from the rock slab and rush to the next room. There you find a boy, just about P.J.'s size and age, seated on the floor.

Turn to page 14.

You break stride, dropping back just as the girl reaches for you. You grab her outstretched arm and burst forward, pulling her by the wrist and whirling her around. Although the girl doesn't fall, she loses precious seconds regaining her balance.

You cross the finish line as the winner. The blond girl comes in last and is led away by a group of guards.

"What will happen to her?" you ask one of the other runners.

"She will be sacrificed tonight for failing to salute the spirits of the dead with her excellence," he replies.

You begin to wonder if—in some way—you can help the girl escape her fate. As you watch the High Priest begin the ceremonies that night, you suddenly come up with a plan. The blond girl is brought toward the fire blazing in front of the altar. But before she reaches it, you leap in front of the High Priest and light two matches from your backpack. The crowd—startled by your control of fire—is momentarily stunned. You grab the girl's hand and run for the forest. When you're safely hidden, she thanks you and leaves to find her family.

Turn to page 47.

46

As you watch, a boy approaches you. You try
to avoid him, but he obviously means to speak to
you. "Kelb," he says, "it is time for you to run.
This is your event." He pulls you with him to the
track. Ahead of you, the lanes seem to stretch forever. Drums begin to beat, and the crowd forgets
the past victory, concentrating on the new con-
test.

The other runners are lean and muscular. You
doubt that you could ever win this race. But if you
don't run, you might meet the fate of the terrified
runner you just saw.

If you run the race, turn to page 62.

*If you try to get out of running,
turn to page 25.*

Late that night, you approach the altar again and take out the three mystic stones. You expose them to the moonlight and their power takes hold, hurling you forward in time. The first person you see is P.J.

"You won't believe what happened to me," you tell him. He listens eagerly, and then says, "It happened to me, too!" P.J. tells you an amazing story of fierce tribal battles at Stonehenge. Together, the two of you realize that you've stumbled on one of the greatest discoveries of mankind —you've traveled through time!

The End

You remain near Stonehenge as the night wears on. Finally, Merlin comes rushing from a group of huts at the edge of the plain. "Thank goodness you waited," he says. "There is terrible trouble afoot. Aurelius is turning my monument into a fortress! He is going to build walls where I have built doors. And I strongly suspect that he has other schemes in mind as well. We must leave here."

Raising his arms, Merlin begins to rise. When he's about ten feet above the ground, he suddenly looks down. "Oh, I should have told you," he says. "When I brought you back in time, I gave you certain powers. You can fly. You can also transform yourself into other creatures should the need arise."

You stare at Merlin with amazement. "Come now," he says. "Don't shilly-shally. We have to get along."

Turn to page 52.

You place the mug on the table.

"Go ahead," Malcolm urges. "Drink."

"No, I don't think so," you say, pushing the mug across the table. Malcolm glares at you and storms from the hut.

You look out the door and see that you've been left under guard. The night passes slowly. Finally, you get an idea.

"Guard!" you call out. "Are you thirsty?" He looks at you suspiciously and then turns to enter the hut. As he walks through the door, you trip him—and run for your life into the village.

You sneak around the village all night looking for Merlin. As the sun rises you head toward the forest at the edge of the plain. You haven't gone far when one of Aurelius's guards stops you.

"What are you doing here?" he asks. Luckily, he doesn't recognize you as the person who had been placed under guard. He signals to several other guards, and they bring you to a group of people sitting in a large cart.

A woman leans over to you and whispers, "They are looking for spies. You had better stall— tell them you are a workman or a traveler."

*If you tell them you're a workman,
turn to page 57.*

*If you tell them you're a traveler,
turn to page 59.*

Merlin closes his eyes, and one by one, the huge stones begin to float through the air. Slowly they begin to spin, like planets in orbit. The stones spin around Merlin—whirling, tilting, gyrating. Suddenly Merlin's eyes open, and the stones fall to the ground with an enormous crash.

"It will take hundreds of years to straighten that out," he laughs. "And by then, Aurelius will long be gone. But you, my friend, will be able to use Stonehenge in your time. Perhaps you will bring it to the glory I once imagined for it.

"Now, before you return," Merlin continues, "you might like to see more of the world in the year 1800 B.C. I could take you to see my people the Druids, the ancient Greeks, even. What do you say?"

At that, you and Merlin rise into the sky, flying toward new adventures in ancient times.

The End

You grab P.J.'s hand and stare. The two of you have taken on the same rainbow tint that's in the rocks! You feel trapped, unable to escape the force pulling you into Stonehenge.

Suddenly you and P.J. are hurled into the air. You whirl around the stones as if you were on some kind of crazy merry-go-round. The chanting grows louder, and the light becomes brighter and brighter. P.J.'s hand is slipping away! A thousand different colors have taken over your mind. You become dizzy, and then the colors black out.

Turn to page 55.

Raising your arms, you begin to float above the ground. It takes you a little while—you keep rolling over or leaning too far to one side—but soon you're flying!

With Merlin leading the way, you fly over the tops of the trees and deep into the forest. He lands next to a large tree, places his hand on the trunk, and pulls open a door! "We'll rest here," he says. You step inside the tree and follow Merlin to an underground cave containing a simple one-room dwelling.

Turn to page 79.

A large bearded man shakes you awake. It seems to be morning. As you regain your senses, you see that the man is wearing a rough, burlap tunic. Tools made of wood and stone hang from his thick leather belt. He speaks to you in very guttural tones that somehow sound familiar. Confused, you stand up slowly. Only then do you notice that your body and clothing have changed completely—you've become someone else!

Turn to page 85.

"Thanks for the advice," you say to Joanne. "Show me to the guest tent."

Joanne brings you to a small tent tucked between hers and the supply tent. "You might get asked to help with some of the chores here," she says, "but I think it'll suit your purposes."

By the end of the day, "some of the chores" have turned into an endless string of tasks.

When you get to bed you can barely keep your eyes open. You quickly fall into a deep sleep. And you dream. A young man dressed in long, flowing robes of fine silk beckons to you, calling, "Get up and come to the altar. I need your help."

Then a hand grips your shoulder and shakes you. You see Joanne standing above your bed. "Hey, wake up!" she says. "You were screaming in your sleep. What was it? A nightmare?"

Turn to page 60.

"I'm a stonemason. I'm looking for work at the monument," you tell the guard. Immediately you are placed on a work crew to cut elaborate designs into the stones.

You've never really done stonecutting before, and it's hard work. Using a small ax, you spend the day chipping away at an enormous boulder, copying the designs of a mason next to you.

While you are working, you overhear the foreman telling one of the masons, "Aurelius is sending that crazy wizard Merlin away. Perhaps now we can get this thing built and move on."

You know that if Merlin is sent away, you may never return to your own time. Just then a voice behind you calls, "Quick, follow me!" You turn to see Merlin, and the guards allow you to go with him.

"Everything has gone wrong," Merlin explains. "I cannot even show you what I brought you back in time for. You must return to your own time now. Are you ready?"

Go on to the next page.

You nod and say goodbye to Merlin.

You feel yourself fading away through time. Your body becomes light, and everything around you turns dim. Suddenly, the environment around you begins to take shape; the light becomes stronger, and you feel your body becoming heavier.

You're sitting on a horse, dressed as a knight! A crowd is shouting all around you. In your hand, you're holding a long, heavy lance.

You look up. About a hundred yards ahead of you, the biggest horse and rider you have ever seen charges toward you. Your horse begins to gallop.

Oh, no! What has Merlin done? You're in the middle of a medieval jousting match!

The End

"I'm a traveler from the north. I've lost my way," you tell the guard.

"Well, go on, then," he snaps, "and do not let us find you here again!"

For most of that day you roam through the forest searching for Merlin. Finally, just before nightfall, you work your way back to Stonehenge. You hope you'll find him there.

As you near the monument, you notice some activity at the edge of the clearing. Two men are coming out of a hut, carrying a large sack between them. You sneak closer—one of the men is Malcolm; the other must be Aurelius! Carefully, they load the sack onto a cart.

It occurs to you that the sack is large enough to hold a human being—and that Merlin might be inside!

*If you follow Malcolm and Aurelius,
turn to page 69.*

*If you continue to search for Merlin around
Stonehenge, turn to page 71.*

60

Starting over from the beginning, you tell Joanne about your dream. With every detail her eyes become wider, and she looks more excited. By the time you finish, Joanne seems to be in a trance. Abruptly, she snaps out of it and laughs nervously.

"Just like I said," she mumbles, hurrying to get out of your tent, "I love dreams. They're so . . . crazy!" With that, she's out your door like a shot.

You sit in your tent, puzzled by Joanne's hasty exit. Perhaps Joanne knows something that you don't!

You get up off your cot and walk out into the cool night. The camp is silent. Looking around at the dark tents, you begin to feel foolish for believing in this dream business. But there's a nagging doubt in your mind. . . .

If you walk toward the altar stone, as the dream suggested, turn to page 23.

If you return to your tent and go back to sleep, turn to page 65.

All you want is to get that spear away from your throat. "No, I am not with the Beakers," you answer.

"Then who *are* you with?" the girl demands. "I have never seen you before."

"I'm just a traveler," you say. "I'm lost. Please let me go!"

"I will let you go this time," she says, "but if I ever see you again, I will kill you."

You scurry down the river bank for about a mile. When you feel certain you haven't been followed, you head back to Stonehenge.

Standing in the monument, the moon glowing above, you remove the stones from your pouch and approach the altar stone. You lay the stones on the ground and watch as the colors appear. The stones rise from the ground, and the singing begins.

Turn to page 66.

You'll run the race and give it your best. The runners are all barefoot, so you take off your sandals. You're surprised at how soft the track is.

The starter holds his hand up, and the runners crouch low, waiting for his signal. The crowd is silent.

With a crack of a wooden staff on stone, the race begins. You forge forward, leaving the others far behind. Then you realize—they must be pacing themselves. You have no idea how long the course is, so you drop back to keep a comfortable second place behind the leader, a tall blond girl.

After what seems well over a mile, the track begins to curve. A small crowd, the first people you've seen since the starting line, cheers you on. The blond girl gets a hearty cheer. You wonder if she's the favorite.

The race goes into the home stretch. Your lungs are bursting, and your legs are aching. But a vision of the horrible fate met by the loser keeps you going.

Just past a rise up ahead, you catch sight of the finish line. The crowd is going crazy. The track drops into a small valley. You use the incline to gain on the leader. Suddenly, she reaches over to you and tries to pull you down! The others behind you ignore it. You dodge the girl, but she keeps coming toward you.

If you try to fight back, turn to page 44.

If you try to avoid her, running as best you can, turn to page 106.

"We'll join the raiding party," you say, looking at P.J. and wondering if either of you will ever be able to make sense of this situation.

Starn leads you in the direction of a group of men who are armed with spears, slings, and bronze shields. The raiders leave the Priestess's fortress and break into small bands. You and Starn travel into the forest on your own.

After about a quarter of a mile, Starn spots the Huntsmen's camp. The camp is nothing more than a dozen tents made from animal skins. But there is one tent set off from the rest of the camp. "That is where they have the Priestess," Starn says. "Wait here. I will get the others." Before you can argue, Starn is running.

You wait a while, and then when Starn doesn't return, you carefully head back to the fortress. On your way, you meet P.J.

"The Huntsmen have invaded the fortress," P.J. tells you. "The raiding party has been ordered back there. But I found out something *else*—the Priestess has our stones!"

If you try to rescue the Priestess, you could be killed. But you could also be killed fighting the Huntsmen and never get a chance to return to your own time.

*If you try to rescue the Priestess,
turn to page 90.*

*If you head back to the fortress,
turn to page 36.*

You go back to sleep, and again you dream of the young man. "Come now to the altar stone," he says. This time you wake up and leave your tent.

Not quite sure what is dream and what is real, you walk sleepily through the camp until you reach the center of Stonehenge. There, standing in front of the altar stone, is the young man you dreamed of—if you've really stopped dreaming!

"Who are you?" you ask, amazed that your voice sounds so clear. Perhaps this isn't a dream after all!

Turn to page 67.

Suddenly you are thrown to the ground. Looking up, you see the girl. So she *has* been following you! You leap to your feet and try to push her away, but she's stronger than anyone you've ever fought. She throws you to the ground again and grabs the middle stone. With tremendous speed, she is hurled into the air. You watch helplessly as she disappears into time.

Now you're trapped!

The End

"I called you because you are a writer, and I have a story," the young man begins. "Perhaps you have heard of me. I am called Merlin. Years from now, when I am much older, I will befriend a young boy named Arthur, and our days will be well recorded. For now, I am a wizard in the court of Aurelius, Lord of Northern Britain. It is for him that I created what you call Stonehenge, this place of deep power. But Aurelius now plans to use the ring of stones for his own evil ends, and not for the reasons I built it."

"But why did you come to me?" you ask. "Why did you come to my time?"

Merlin sighs. "To tell you the truth, I am not very good at this time travel. I just ended up here. I am pretty sure we can get to my time safely, though. Will you come back with me?"

Turn to page 38.

You walk with P.J. to the inner ring of Stonehenge. Above you the moon is growing darker as the earth casts its shadow.

In the middle of the monument, the eclipsed moon has produced a laserlike pinspot of light. The bright spot wavers on the ground. Suddenly you and P.J. are caught in the light. There is a brief flash, like a bolt of lightning, and the Stonehenge you once stood within is gone—replaced by a half-constructed monument, bathed in sunlight! Outside the monument, you hear hundreds of voices chanting. You look around. P.J. is gone!

Turn to page 70.

You follow Malcolm and Aurelius as they drive the cart into the woods and up a long, steep path. After about an hour, they reach a clearing. It appears that they're waiting for someone. You move closer, trying to hear what they're saying. But you can't get close enough without risking being seen. You crouch behind a tree and wait.

After quite a while, a small man who looks like a gypsy comes into the clearing. You watch while he talks with Aurelius. Malcolm loads the sack from their cart onto the back of the gypsy's horse.

You've been sitting in one position for so long that your body has become stiff. You try to shift your weight, but instead you fall completely over. Malcolm's head snaps up. Then he strides toward you.

Turn to page 110.

You seem to be in the middle of a parade. Hundreds of people, wearing feather headdresses and painted animal skins, circle the monument in a line. Looking down, you see that your clothing has changed completely. All you wear now are a short leather tunic, a pair of moccasins, and a wristband made of leather and animal teeth.

Trying not to call attention to yourself, you join the circling line, all the time looking for P.J. Then you see him—being carried on an ornate bier at the head of the parade! This is crazy!

The procession makes its way into Stonehenge, and P.J. is placed on the throne within the monument. You watch in disbelief as a bronze crown is set on his head.

A man who appears to be something of a High Priest turns to P.J. "The moon has sent you to us, as the prophets predicted," he says. "You are our chieftain now. You must choose the one who will always be at your side." You watch as P.J. scans the eerily silent crowd. He raises his hands in the air and closes his eyes.

You want to break the silence and call out to P.J., but you hesitate. Something inside you warns that you could be letting yourself in for big trouble.

If you call out to P.J., turn to page 73.

If you remain silent, turn to page 88.

You wait until Aurelius and Malcolm leave, then walk toward the hut. Inside a guard stands over Merlin, who has been bound and gagged. You step outside the door and call out, "Help! Help! Aurelius has had a terrible accident. Come quickly!" The guard rushes out, and you dash into the hut.

Untying Merlin, you tell him, "Aurelius left with a big sack."

"He has stolen valuable jewels that belong to the tribe," Merlin says. "But worse than that, he is planning to execute me tomorrow morning. I am afraid I will have to work fast—and you will have to listen well to what I am going to tell you."

With that, Merlin rushes out to Stonehenge. He stands in the center of the stone rings. "This monument," he says, "was designed by me, based on everything I know about the sun, the moon, and the earth. Using the stones from the nearby quarry, I attempted to create a power source on earth. A place where the energy of all three bodies—sun, moon, earth—could be united. A place where man could find the strength to defy gravity, time, and space. But I cannot allow this to come into Aurelius's hands, for he will use that power for evil. I brought you here to this time so that you could begin to know the true meaning of Stonehenge, and bring it to your troubled time."

Turn to page 50.

Your thirst gets the better of you, and you drink from the mug. It's not too bad, so you take a few more sips.

Gradually you become drowsy.

Malcolm comes and stands over you. "Now, tell me exactly who you are. And do not lie!" he commands.

You realize that you've been given some kind of truth serum. You feel terribly weak. You must be in real danger. You try to think of anything *but* what Malcolm wants you to tell him. You wish that you were some kind of animal that could run away from Malcolm!

Turn to page 74.

"P.J.," you call as he descends from the throne. All heads turn to gaze at you. You've broken the sacred silence of the ceremony! As P.J. walks away, he sneaks a quick but angry look at you, as if to say, "Don't get us both in trouble!"

Seeing that you won't get any help from P.J., you turn to leave the ceremony. But before you can leave the monument, two of the High Priest's guards seize you. You are taken to a stone prison.

That evening the door to your cell opens. P.J. enters with the High Priest and the one whom he named as his helper that afternoon.

"Do you know this person, mighty Chieftain?" the High Priest asks.

From the way P.J. acts you can tell that he's not free to admit he knows you. Fear grips you as he answers, "I have never seen this one before."

Turn to page 111.

Before you can even wonder how it happened, you find yourself turned into a rabbit! You scoot between Malcolm's feet and out the door, the young man chasing after you. He manages to kick you so hard you faint. Everything goes black.

Go on to the next page.

When you come to, you look around. It looks as if you're back in your tent at the student camp in Stonehenge. Except that everything around you is ten times larger than it used to be. You've returned to your own time as a rabbit!

What has Merlin done? You hop around frantically, trying to switch back to human form, but you remain a rabbit.

That night, Joanne comes into your tent with P.J. "What a mystery," she says. "No one knows where he went. He just disappeared." You jump in front of her, trying to signal in some way that it's *you* in this furry body.

"Hey, look at this," Joanne calls to P.J. She picks you up and begins to rub your nose. "What a cute rabbit!" She snuggles her face next to yours. "Would you like to be my pet, rabbit? C'mon, I'll get you some carrots."

The End

"But will the Huntsmen keep their promise?" Osin asks.

Without thinking, you shift your weight and accidentally step on some loose rocks. Osin and Beltan look up at you.

"Well, Auric," Osin says. "Have you arrived early today to make up for the time you lost yesterday?" You nod, and he continues to speak. "Perhaps Auric can help us with our problem."

"Of course!" Beltan says, clapping his hands together. "Why did I not think of that! A stonecutter, with access to the Priestess. Auric, how would you like to be paid handsomely for a very small, very important job?"

"What kind of job?" you ask.

"Why, as a spy!" Osin answers.

*If you agree to spy for the men,
turn to page 103.*

*If you say that you won't be a spy,
turn to page 40.*

"I think you are good people," you tell Soren, "but I just don't believe fighting is going to help you. I'm going to travel on."

The next morning, Soren leads you to the edge of the Beaker camp. "Take good care of yourself," he says. Then he turns back to his people.

You wind your way deeper into the forest. But just before you lose sight of the Beakers, you stop.

The Beaker camp is filled with chaotic activity. The men and women are painting their faces, playing drums, attaching sharp flint and bronze blades to spears, practicing combat moves with their daggers. You remain hidden and watch as they gather to march toward Stonehenge.

As they march you follow from a distance. The Beakers form into a line directly in front of the Huntsmen's fortress and charge forward.

Turn to page 19.

You remain in the Beaker camp. The next day, you watch as they prepare for battle. Their weapons and plans are primitive, and you can tell that many will be wounded or die in the planned head-on attack.

"I can't sit here and watch you prepare for this slaughter," you tell Soren. "Let me show you how you can protect yourselves better."

You teach them some battle tricks that only a person from another time could know. You inspect their weapons and then show them how to make bows and slingshots, how to form lines for loading and firing, and how to use strategy instead of rushing in a crowd toward Stonehenge.

When the Beakers are ready to march into battle, Soren approaches you. "We have decided that you should lead us." You know this could be dangerous, but you accept the assignment anyway.

Turn to page 82.

When you wake up the next morning, Merlin is gone. You open the door in the tree and look outside. At first you see nothing except other trees. Then you notice a narrow path. You follow the path through the forest, but there's no sign of Merlin.

You are about to head back toward the cave when one of Aurelius's guards stops you. "What is your business on this path?" he demands. Before you can answer, he signals several other guards. They grab you roughly and take you to a cart.

There are other prisoners in the cart. One man leans over to you and whispers, "They are looking for spies. Stall for time—tell them you are a workman or a traveler."

If you tell the guard you're a workman,
turn to page 57.

If you tell the guard you're a traveler,
turn to page 59.

Leaving P.J. behind, you turn from Stonehenge and run back to the camp for help. Just as you reach the tents, though, P.J. rushes up behind you.

"Where are you going?" he asks, puffing and gasping for breath.

"I was going to get help," you reply.

"You don't need to do that," P.J. says calmly. "It was—"

"What's going on here?" Joanne interrupts. "What's all this noise?"

"Nothing that would interest you," P.J. says matter-of-factly. "There appears to be a paranormal disturbance occurring in the monument. I felt it would be best to come back here and put a team together to observe it, although our friend here," he says, nodding toward you, "only cares about reporting, and wanted to take it on all alone."

Go on to the next page.

"That isn't what happened at all!" you try to explain. "But if we do want to observe it, we'd better hurry."

"Okay, I'll go get some of the others," Joanne says. "I'll meet you back here in fifteen minutes."

Joanne rushes off to her tent. P.J. says to you, "That's a good idea. I think I'll get some equipment from my tent, too." In a flash, he's gone.

Something tells you that the *last* place P.J. is heading for is his tent.

If you wait for Joanne, turn to page 32.

If you return to Stonehenge, hoping to head off P.J., turn to page 5.

The Beakers descend from their camp in the forest and surround the Huntsmen's village at Stonehenge. You lead the charge as spears, arrows, rocks, and pellets fly all around you. Suddenly you feel a sharp pain. Your leg has been hit by a spear!

You can no longer walk. You lie on the ground while the battle rages on around you.

Turn to page 24.

You try to walk, but your head is ringing. Above you is a large platform made of logs, surrounding two of the enormous Stonehenge slabs.

"Someone help Auric!" the man calls. He speaks in the same language you heard coming from the rocks, and you're amazed that you can understand everything he says.

Several young people help you to your feet. Something rattles in the pouch tied around your waist. Reaching in, you feel the three stones that brought you to this place.

"Here are your tools," a young girl says, handing you a leather pouch. "We can finish carving the top of the stone tomorrow. You have had a nasty fall." A boy your age holds out his hand to you. He has bright red hair and an impish grin. "Come, Auric," he says. "I will walk with you down the road."

Go on to the next page.

As you walk from the monument you see that Stonehenge is in a very late stage of construction. The altar stone stands within the inner ring, and the trilithons are being completed.

Suddenly, you remember—P.J.! Where is he?

"Well, Auric," your escort says when you reach a fork in the road, "here is where I turn for home. I will see you tomorrow." He seems to know where he's going, but you have no idea where you are.

If you tell the boy that you don't know where your home is, and risk his realizing that you are not Auric, turn to page 43.

If you decide to bluff your way through the village, turn to page 13.

"We'll stay and defend the fortress," you tell Starn. "Just tell us what to do."

Starn leads you to a small cave dug into the earthen circle around the monument. "You will be brought spears, daggers, and other weapons that need repair," he tells you. "Fix them as fast as possible with those tools there, and return them to the warriors."

You and P.J. go to work. Crazy as this situation is, P.J. remains the archeologist. "It's amazing how elaborate their tools are," he says. "They appear clumsy, but when you pick them up you realize they're perfectly fitted to the human hand."

"Is that all you can think of—"

You break off as the cry of battle rises. The camp is being overrun again—but this time the Huntsmen have succeeded in luring the Priestess's best warriors into the fight. The battle rages. Then Huntsmen break through the fortress's defenses!

One of the Huntsmen rushes into the cave and brutally seizes you. He drags you to an open area where the tribal warriors of the Priestess are being held prisoner.

Turn to page 102.

You remain silent. At the end of the ceremony you follow the crowd to a settlement in the forest near Stonehenge. Their homes are thatched cottages, constructed from the trees and vines. As far as you can tell, P.J. has been taken to a fortress near the monument, which serves as the chief's home.

For a while you roam around the village, then an older woman stops you. "I do not recognize you," she says. "Where do you come from?"

You think fast. "I came for the crowning of the new chief," you reply. "But my journey back is long, and I'm looking for a place to stay for the night."

"I have taken strangers in before," the woman says. "You may stay in my home for one night, provided you help with my work in the morning."

Turn to page 92.

The three of you head toward the monument. In the center of the inner ring, you lay the three stones on the ground. Slowly, they absorb the moonlight and then take on the colorful hues you saw when you first traveled through time. The stones lift from the ground, and the two end stones begin revolving.

You grasp P.J.'s hand and reach for the middle stone. "Better to stick with what we know," you say. You become dizzy and lose consciousness.

When you wake up, you are sitting in the middle of Stonehenge. You stand up, and see P.J. lying not far away from you. His eyes are wide open and a look of amazement is on his face.

"That can't have been real," P.J. says.

Suddenly you hear Joanne's voice. "Where have you been?" she cries. "We thought you had died. You've been gone for two whole days!"

"Two days?" you laugh. "More like four thousand years!"

The End

90

You and P.J. agree to try to rescue the Priestess. Reaching the Huntsmen's camp, you see several guards standing outside the tent that is set off from the rest of the camp. "I bet that's where they're keeping her," P.J. says.

"It is," you answer, bending to pick up a rock. You each gather a handful of rocks and throw them about fifty yards away. When the guards hear the rocks falling, they rush to see what's happening.

P.J. waits in the forest while you run for the tent. Inside you find the Priestess; her hands and feet are bound with thick ropes. Quickly you untie her. "Follow me," you whisper. The two of you rush toward the forest—but not before two guards see you and set off in hot pursuit.

Turn to page 95.

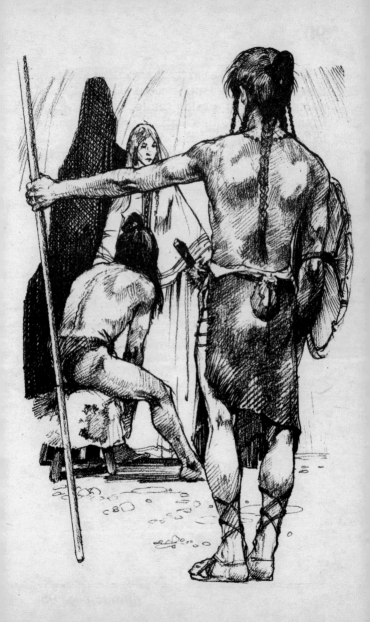

The woman, whose name is Mera, takes you into her home, which is filled with iron and bronze sculptures. You remember how rare these metals were in the past. "You must be a person of great wealth," you say.

"Not at all," Mera replies. "I am just the village smith. What you see here are some of my wares. They will leave my home whenever I can sell them."

The next day you help Mera at her forge, hauling raw iron and bronze from the storage area to her work area. As you're working you see P.J. and the High Priest walking past Mera's home. You run to him, calling, "P.J.! P.J.!" but he doesn't even look at you. Disgusted, you return to Mera's.

Turn to page 26.

Walking away from Stonehenge, you search for Merlin in a small gathering of huts at the edge of the plain. Without warning, an armed young man carrying a spear approaches you menacingly. "Get out of here," he snarls as he pushes his spear toward you. "Leave now, before you are jailed."

"I'm looking for Merlin," you tell him.

The young man stops for a moment, and takes a long, careful look at you. "I am Malcolm, son of Aurelius, Lord of Northern Britain. Perhaps you should come with me." He sounds a little more friendly. You hope he'll take you somewhere with food and water.

Turn to page 96.

Over the next few months, you live with Caleb's family. Life here is very different from the one you knew in the twentieth century. Your life is centered around the crops. Depending on the season, you and Tyn plant, harvest, or trade them at the cursus. You make many new friends, and feel as though you've found a home. You forget about your story for *Tightwire*. You nearly forget about the twentieth century.

One day, years after your arrival, there is a great deal of excitement at the cursus.

"What's going on?" you ask Caleb.

"The astronomers have predicted that the moon will darken tonight," Caleb answers. "It is a time of high magic at the stone ring."

"Remember the magic I told you about when I first came here?" you ask.

"Yes, I do," he answers. "And you are right to think that tonight you will be able to travel through time. You are welcome to stay with us, but we will understand if you feel you want to go back."

Turn to page 98.

You and the Priestess run deep into the woods. Small trees and branches snap at your face and ankles. The Priestess points to your left. "That way," she says. "There is a secret trail. No one will find us there. We will be safe until we reach the fortress." You follow the trail, hoping P.J.'s okay.

You've almost reached Stonehenge when a band of Huntsmen leaps from the brush. There's no chance to escape. They capture you and bring you both back to their camp.

You and the Priestess wait out the night, listening to the sounds of battle coming from the forest.

The next day the Warlord of the Huntsmen strides into the tent where you're being held. "Well, Priestess," he says, "I have some bad news for you. Your beloved Ring of the Moon is now ours. And we must offer thanks to the sun. We have decided to honor you and your young friend with the privilege of being our first sacrifice. Tonight you will be burned."

The End

Malcolm leads you to a large hut. "This is my home," he says as you enter through thick oak doors. The room is simple—a table, chairs, two hay mattresses on the floor, and a fireplace. "Have a seat," he tells you. "Would you care for something to drink?"

"That would be great," you answer. Malcolm leaves you in the hut and goes out. A short while later, he returns with a mug of steaming liquid. As he hands it to you, you glance at his eyes. Something is very wrong! He's waiting too eagerly for you to take a sip.

Go on to the next page.

If you drink from the mug, turn to page 72.

*If you don't drink from the mug,
turn to page 49.*

You spend the rest of the day considering your decision. Finally, you talk with Tyn.

"We are very good friends," Tyn says, "but I have often thought about what it would be like to be you. I, myself, would go back to my time. That is where you came from, and where your destiny will always be."

That night, as the earth's shadow crosses the moon, you turn to Caleb, Tyn, and their family.

"Thank you all very much. I'll never forget you," you tell them. Before you begin crying, you walk toward the center of the ring. There you place on the ground the three stones that brought you to this time. The magic begins again. You take one last look back and begin to travel through time, toward the twentieth century.

The End

A Beaker man comes up to you and leads you to his campfire. "I am Soren," he says, "and this is my family."

You ask them about their tribe and about the people building the monument.

"We are of the Beaker tribe. The men you saw are Huntsmen," Soren explains. "The Huntsmen took control of the great stone ring from a gentle tribe led by a Priestess of the Moon. They are using its great power to make war on others. Now, they are fighting with our tribe because we will not give our food to their chief. Many other tribes give them food out of fear, but we refuse to be afraid."

Go on to the next page.

100

As Soren continues to speak others gather around him. "We are nomads who believe in every family raising its own food, making its own goods, and then gathering to trade. We also believe, as others do not, in burying our dead alone, instead of in large graves of many people. We believe that we live our lives alone, and so we should go to our rest alone." At this, he pauses. "I am afraid that tomorrow many from both our tribes will go to their rest," he says sorrowfully.

As Soren talks of the battle ahead, you begin to grow restless. This is much more than you bargained for when you came into the camp. You wonder if there's a way to avoid the battle and still protect yourself from being killed in a case of mistaken identity.

*If you stay in the Beaker camp,
turn to page 78.*

If you move on, turn to page 77.

"You are not a stone carver," the Priestess says, "any more than your friend here"—with a nod to P.J.—"is a merchant. But I must congratulate both of you for having so successfully deceived my tribesmen. I, myself, have had similar experiences, traveling through time and living in other realities.

"The ground we stand on now is hallowed," she continues. "The gods use it for their own purposes. You two must be part of their plans, and it is our duty to discover what those plans are. I want you to remain here as my guests today. Tonight, we will test the powers of the moon on your being, and on these stones you brought with you."

That night the Priestess summons you and P.J. from your cell. "If you truly have the power to travel in time," she says, handing you the stones, "I will allow you to go free. But if you have lost this power, you will be killed as spies."

Turn to page 89.

Late that night, a shrill whistle pierces the silence. The warriors around you immediately cover themselves. You and P.J. follow their example. Boulders and rocks fly through the air, killing many of the Huntsmen. The Priestess's raiding party has staged a counterattack! But the Huntsmen hold their ground.

The next morning, you and P.J. are summoned to the center of Stonehenge where the Warlord of the Huntsmen waits for you. The Warlord is a large man, draped in furs and animal skins. As you enter the ring, he opens his hand, revealing your three stones.

"I have heard about you," he says, "and about the power in these stones. I believe the source of their power is the sun, not the moon. Now I will show you how to use their magic properly."

The Warlord places the small stones on the ground and begins to chant. In the bright sunlight, the stones begin to rise from the ground. The Warlord grabs the middle stone. Instantly his flesh seems to glow red-hot. He continues to chant, speaking faster and faster—then he rises into the air and disappears!

Turn to page 107.

"Okay," you say to the men. "I will spy for you—on one condition."

"What would that be?" Osin asks.

"That you stay close by me, for my protection," you say.

At this, Beltan laughs. "A good deal," he answers. "We will start in the Priestess's temple. Whatever you hear, report back to Osin."

You and Osin walk down the broad avenue to a group of wood-and-mud huts a few hundred yards away from the monument. A thick fortresslike wall surrounds the small village. Osin thinks you know where you are going, but you very subtly allow him to show you the way by his movements.

At the temple, a large stone-and-glass structure, the guards allow you to pass inside when you say you're working for the Priestess. Osin waits outside.

Turn to page 105.

104

As the men move closer you jump behind a clump of bushes and hide.

"The Beaker tribe is camping nearby," one of the men says.

"They are all around us," the other answers. "We must always be on the lookout."

The two men pass, not seeing you. That night, you watch from your hideout on the river bank. Campfires dot the plain around Stonehenge. You smell meat cooking, and hunger grips you.

Suddenly a hand clasps your shoulder. You whirl around to see a girl, just about your age, standing behind you. She points a spear directly at your throat.

"Are you with the Beakers?" she asks.

You have no way of knowing if the girl is with the Beaker tribe or with those who are building Stonehenge. But you do know that your life depends on your answer.

If you say you are not with the Beakers, turn to page 61.

If you say you've never heard of the Beakers, turn to page 29.

A guard leads you into a massive hall. There, sitting on a splendid throne of bronze and amber, is the most beautiful woman you've ever seen. She is arrayed in the finest silks, and wearing bronze necklaces and medallions. Even more amazing is that seated right in front of her is a boy who looks just like P.J.!

Before you can say a word, you are searched. The guard discovers your three stones and takes them away. Then the Priestess dismisses the guard.

Turn to page 101.

With all the strength in your legs, you dodge the tall blond girl. She pursues you, and you rush from side to side, straining to gain sight of the finish line.

As you head up the hill and out of the valley, the girl pulls slightly ahead of you. Your strength is practically gone, and the hill is draining the last of your power. Your lungs feel as if they're on fire. Every pore in your skin is bathed in white heat.

Suddenly, the girl breaks far ahead of you. In frustration, you lose your pace, and the other runners sprint ahead.

You cross the finish line last. Two guards drag you into a stone building, where a group of athletes are sitting on the floor.

"What's going on here?" you ask.

"You don't know?" one of them says, amazed at your ignorance. "We're going to be sacrificed tonight, at sunset."

You finger the stones in your pouch—the stones that need moonlight to work. There won't be a chance to test their power again. Your fate has been sealed.

The End

With the stones gone, there's no hope of your returning to the twentieth century. You and P.J. live out long and fruitful lives under the rule of the Huntsmen, although your days are filled with the violence of an ever-warring tribe.

One day, when you are old, you try to inscribe in stone what has happened to you, and what you know of how Stonehenge came to be built. You hope that some day, someone will find your words and understand.

The End

You put on the mask and place the tunic over your shoulders. Looking around the cursus, you see a group of others dressed as you are. You walk up to them.

The group watches the next event in silence. After the race, you listen as they talk among themselves. It appears that you are wearing the face and shield of a soldier who died in a recent battle. These people believe that when the dead are put to rest, games and rituals should be held for their spirits. In this way, the dead will know that they are still respected and loved.

Go on to the next page.

Throughout the day you follow the group from event to event. The funeral games seem a lot like modern track and field events. But they become very different as the sun begins to set. Your group gathers around a fire where, under the direction of a High Priest, you each burn your mask and shield.

After the masks are burned the High Priest calls for another ritual to begin. You can scarcely believe your eyes when you see the losers of the day's funeral games led to the fire. They are to be sacrificed to the souls which, according to the High Priest, "they could not honor with their excellence." You watch horrified as they are hurled into the fire.

Still shaken, you return to the altar stone late that night. You take the three stones that brought you back in time from your pack and wait for the moon to cast its light on them. Soon the stones begin to work their magic.

When you wake up, P.J. is standing next to you. "Where have you been?" he asks. "We've been looking for you all day."

You begin to explain about your trip through time. P.J. listens and then shrugs his shoulders. "I thought reporters were supposed to stick to the facts," he says, "but *that* sounds like pure fiction to me."

The End

Instantly, you're up and running. Malcolm takes off after you. Leaping over rocks and fallen trees, you run as hard as you can to evade him. But he gains on you. You veer to the right, then double back toward the clearing to throw him off. The woods grow quiet. You've lost him.

Trying to catch your breath, you slow to a walk. Suddenly you hear someone right behind you. Just as suddenly you feel Malcolm's dagger in your back. As you lie dying, you hear the young man's laughter in the distance.

The End

"You are the chief now, sent to us by the gods," the High Priest tells him. "You must be careful not to stain your purity by associating with commoners."

The High Priest leads P.J. and the other boy out of the cell. As they leave you hear the High Priest issue a command to the guard:

"Execute the prisoner at dawn."

The End

ABOUT THE AUTHOR

FRED GRAVER lives in New York City. When he isn't writing, or editing the *National Lampoon,* he's listening to his two children, Joshua and Claire, who give him good ideas for adventure books.

ABOUT THE ILLUSTRATOR

LESLIE MORRILL is a designer and illustrator whose work has won him numerous awards. He has illustrated over thirty books for children, including the Bantam Classics edition of *The Wind in the Willows;* for the Bantam Skylark Choose Your Own Adventure series, *Indian Trail* by R. A. Montgomery; and for the Choose Your Own Adventure series, *Lost on the Amazon* by R. A. Montgomery. His work has also appeared frequently in *Cricket* magazine. A graduate of the Boston Museum School of Fine Arts, Mr. Morrill lives near Boston, Massachusetts.

DO YOU LOVE CHOOSE YOUR OWN ADVENTURE®?

**Let your younger brothers and sisters
in on the fun.**

You know how great CHOOSE YOUR OWN ADVEN-TURE® books are to read and reread. But did you know that there are CHOOSE YOUR OWN ADVEN-TURE® books for younger kids too? They're just as thrilling as the CHOOSE YOUR OWN ADVENTURE® books you read and they're filled with the same kinds of decisions and different ways for the stories to end—but they're shorter with more illustrations and come in a larger, easier-to-read size.

So get your younger brothers and sisters and any-one else you know between the ages of seven and nine in on the fun by introducing them to the exciting world of CHOOSE YOUR OWN ADVENTURE.® They're on sale wherever Bantam paperbacks are sold.

AV10

CHOOSE YOUR OWN ADVENTURE

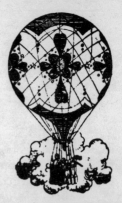

"You'll want all the books in the exciting Choose Your Own Adventure series. Each book takes you through dozens of fantasy adventures—under the sea, in a space colony, into the past—in which *you* are the main character. What happens next in the story depends on the choices *you* make, and *only you* can decide how the story ends!"